ISLINGTON

Please return this item on or before the last date stamped below or you may be liable to overdue charges. To renew an item call the number below, or access the online catalogue at www.islington.gov.uk/libraries. You will need your library membership number and PIN number.

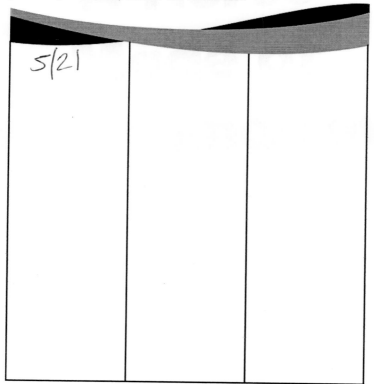

5/21

Islington Libraries

020 7527 6900   **www.islington.gov.uk/libraries**

Level 10 – White

Helpful Hints for Reading at Home

The focus phonemes (units of sound) used throughout this series are in line with the order in which your child is taught at school. This offers a consistent approach to learning whether reading at home or in the classroom.

HERE ARE SOME COMMON WORDS THAT YOUR CHILD MIGHT FIND TRICKY:

water	where	would	know	thought	through	couldn't
laughed	eyes	once	we're	school	can't	our

TOP TIPS FOR HELPING YOUR CHILD TO READ:

- Encourage your child to read aloud as well as silently to themselves.
- Allow your child time to absorb the text and make comments.
- Ask simple questions about the text to assess understanding.
- Encourage your child to clarify the meaning of new vocabulary.

This book focuses on developing independence, fluency and comprehension. It is a white level 10 book band.

A Horse Made of Marshmallow

Written by
William Anthony

Illustrated by
Maia Batumashvili

Chapter One

Fiddlebow Gobfloppers

Mayor Chow was drooling. A crowd of people were starting to gather behind him. His eyes browsed the shelves from left to right and top to bottom. Whistlestop Gumblefizzers, Mini Gingerboards, Dreamy Fluff-Jumbles... It was impossible to choose.

Chow was starting to sweat.
"I'll have five of everything from the top shelf!"
he finally blurted out.
"No problem, Mr Mayor," said a little voice.
"I'll throw in a few Fiddlebow Gobfloppers for
free, too."

Whistle stop
Gumblefizzer

Mini
Gingerboard

Dreamy
Fluff-Jumble

Willow bagged up Mayor Chow's sweets and off he plodded. He'd be back soon – Sweet Dreams was his favourite shop in town.

Willow's father had owned Sweet Dreams before he went away. He left the shop to Willow, because he knew she had an incredible dream. She wanted to turn her town into sweets.

She wanted to make buildings from Jumbo Gingerboards, walk down streets with chocolate cobbles, own a horse made of marshmallow and put on firework shows that rained with sweets.

For now though, Willow was just having fun making sweets and selling them to the townspeople (well, mostly Mayor Chow). She was only seven years old, so she had all the time in the world.

Chapter Two

Bubblepop Choco-Wows

Willow brushed the powdery snow away from the shop door. Today was the launch of her brand-new sweet – the Bubblepop Choco-Wow. It took some tinkering, but it had the chewy pop of bubble gum, the silky taste of chocolate and a perfect dollop of wow-factor.

Willow had barely got through the door when Mayor Chow bumbled in. He was always the first to try Willow's new creations.

He bought the very first Bubblepop Choco-Wow and stuffed it into his mouth.

Round and round went the sweet, slowly chewing and churning. One of Chow's eyebrows raised up as he tried to work out the flavours. Then the other went up when he worked out the flavours were good. Soon, the flavours became so good that his eyebrows had nearly given him a new fringe.

Mayor Chow had to take a deep breath.
"Willow," he gasped. "That sweet is incredible
– a real showstopper! I think it might even be
your best-ever sweet!"
"Wow, do you really think so?" asked Willow.

"How many have you made? I'll buy them all, right here, right now," insisted Chow.
"Over 500! You can't buy them all, Mayor Chow!" said Willow. Chow got his wallet out and emptied out all the money inside. Willow couldn't say no to that.

Over the weeks that followed, Mayor Chow wasn't the only person in town who wanted to stock up on Bubblepop Choco-Wows. Everyone wanted them. Willow was making so much money that she decided to do something quite magical.

Sweet Dreams

Chapter Three

Jumbo Gingerboards

Mayor Chow had quite the shock when he turned up for breakfast at Sweet Dreams. A sign in the door read 'CLOSED'. He peeped through the window, but the shop was empty. It was a real wonder how Chow avoided bursting into tears right there and then.

Willow hadn't closed the shop forever. She was just making a small part of her dream come true.

She started taking out bricks from the walls and replacing them with brownies. She pulled down the wooden shelves and put up chocolate ones. She even swapped the pillows on the seats for candy floss.

In just a few days, Sweet Dreams had become a palace made of sweet, tasty, chocolatey goodness.

Mayor Chow's jaw hit the floor when he saw the new shop. He had never had sweets towering over him before.

"This is just wonderful, Willow! Say, you wouldn't want to rebuild Town Hall as well, would you?" asked Chow.

"Of course I would!" she giggled.
Willow had never built something quite
that big before, but she had all the right
treats – Jumbo Gingerboards for the walls,
Giant Wobbleboppers for the doors and
Swizzlebuttons for the handles.

A few weeks later, the new Town Hall was ready. She was waiting for Mayor Chow to cut the rainbow belt with her, but he was too busy eating the door, so she cut it anyway.
"I declare Town Hall open again!" she beamed.

Chapter Four

Sherbet Skycrackers

Dreams didn't come true for many people in Willow's town, but hers were starting to. She wanted to give everyone a little part of her dream. Willow and Mayor Chow had enough money to rebuild the entire town with sweets!

When spring arrived, Willow started to rebuild the town – house by house, shop by shop, street by street. She made little chocolate cobbles to line the roads and used her Chocolate Nimblesticks to thatch the roofs.

The children were in paradise, the grown-ups loved the incredible sights, Mayor Chow couldn't stop drooling and Willow was glowing with pride. From her father's humble sweet shop, she had brought her dream to life.

Willow wasn't done yet. In her dream, she owned a horse made of marshmallow. She certainly couldn't cover a real horse in marshmallow, so she made one from scratch and called it Gregory. It was perfectly plump and wobbly in every way.

The very same night, Willow was going to complete her dream. She had crafted hundreds of Sherbet Skycrackers – fireworks made with sherbet and sweets – ready for a huge show at the end of the night. Mayor Chow led the countdown.

"Goggles on, everybody!" shouted Willow.
"OK, 3... 2... 1..." yelled Mayor Chow, before pressing the button.

The Skycrackers fizzed and whirled up into the air, exploding in flashes of light. Clouds of sherbet flowed through the air, before sweets showered down on the townspeople. Yellow, pink and red sherbet lit up the night sky, and everybody stuck out their tongues to get a taste of the fizzy goodness.

Everyone was too busy enjoying themselves to realise they'd made a huge mistake.

Something terrible was coming...

Chapter Five

Melt-in-the-Middle Chocopuddles

Sweet Dreams was Willow's real home.

Drip.

Sometimes she would close the shop, just so she could sit on the candy floss pillows and remember all the incredible moments from the last few months.

Drip.

She tucked into a Super-Hollow Chocblock and thought about the day Mayor Chow bought 500 Bubblepop Choco-Wows.
Drip.
Then she thought about the time she actually made herself a horse made of marshmallow.
Drip.

Then she thought about what on earth that dripping sound was...

Willow looked up to see a scary sight. She could see the sky. As the Chocolate Nimblestick roof began to melt away even more, she could see the problem. Summer had arrived.

In no time at all, Willow was drowning in chocolate. She swam to the front door and got out. Behind her, Sweet Dreams collapsed into a pile of sugary goo.

Willow looked around. The world she had made was melting around her. Shops had turned to gloop and houses had slopped to the ground. In the background, Willow heard someone howling. It was Mayor Chow. He was sat in the brown sludge of his much-loved Town Hall, wiping each tear away with a towel. Willow sat down beside him.

"We made a big mistake, Mayor Chow, but everything will be okay," sniffled Willow, as she wiped away a tear of her own.

Chapter Six

A Horse Made of Marshmallow

As summer turned into autumn, the town began to rebuild. Willow was happy to see the town back on its feet, but in the chaos, she had lost her dream. Soon enough, it would become just an old memory.

"Package for Willow," said the postal worker as she walked past. Willow wasn't expecting any mail. She opened the brown parcel and pulled out a letter and a book.

Dear Willow,

I heard about your incredible story. Turning an entire town into sweets should have been impossible, but somehow you made your dream come true.

I'm sorry to hear what happened when summer arrived. You must continue to rebuild your father's shop – I'd love to visit Sweet Dreams one day!

What you did was SO magical that I decided to write a book about it, so children around the world could read about how you made your dream come true.

I've sent you the first copy of the book. I hope you like the title. I called it 'A Horse Made of Marshmallow'.

W. A.

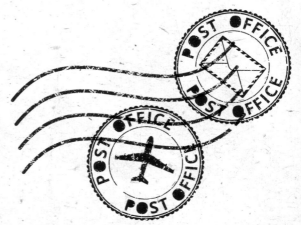

BookLife
Readers

A Horse Made of Marshmallow

SWEET DREAMS

By
William Anthony

Illustrated By
Maia Batumashvili

A Horse Made of Marshmallow

1. What was Mayor Chow's favourite shop in town?

2. Can you describe the Bubblepop Choco–Wow?

3. What did Willow swap the pillows on the seat for?
   (a) Chocolate
   (b) Candy floss
   (c) Bubblegum

4. What were Willow's fireworks called?

5. How do you think Willow felt when the town melted? Have you ever felt like this?

©2020 **BookLife Publishing Ltd.**
King's Lynn, Norfolk PE30 4LS

ISBN 978-1-83927-021-5

A Horse Made of Marshmallow
Written by William Anthony
Illustrated by Maia Batumashvili

An Introduction to BookLife Readers...

Our Readers have been specifically created in line with the London Institute of Education's approach to book banding and are phonetically decodable and ordered to support each phase of the Letters and Sounds document.

Each book has been created to provide the best possible reading and learning experience. Our aim is to share our love of books with children, providing both emerging readers and prolific page-turners with beautiful books that are guaranteed to provoke interest and learning, regardless of ability.

BOOK BAND GRADED using the Institute of Education's approach to levelling.

PHONETICALLY DECODABLE supporting each phase of Letters and Sounds.

EXERCISES AND QUESTIONS to offer reinforcement and to ascertain comprehension.

BEAUTIFULLY ILLUSTRATED to inspire and provoke engagement, providing a variety of styles for the reader to enjoy whilst reading through the series.

AUTHOR INSIGHT:
WILLIAM ANTHONY

Despite his young age, William Anthony's involvement with children's education is quite extensive. He has written over 60 titles with BookLife Publishing so far, across a wide range of subjects. William graduated from Cardiff University with a 1st Class BA (Hons) in Journalism, Media and Culture, creating an app and a TV series, among other things, during his time there.

William Anthony has also produced work for the Prince's Trust, a charity created by HRH The Prince of Wales that helps young people with their professional future. He has created animated videos for a children's education company that works closely with the charity.

This book focuses on developing independence, fluency and comprehension. It is a white level 10 book band.